LUNA

www.holly-webb.com

STRIPES PUBLISHING LIMITED
An imprint of the Little Tiger Group
1 Coda Studios, 189 Munster Road,
London SW6 6AW

www.littletiger.co.uk

This hardback edition first published
in Great Britain in 2020

ISBN: 978-1-78895-215-6

2 4 6 8 10 9 7 5 3 1

HOLLY WEBB
LUNA

Illustrated by Jo Anne Davies

LiTTLE TiGER
LONDON

*With love and admiration for
conservationists still working to
save dancing bears*

~ HOLLY WEBB

Chapter
ONE

Hannah turned round slowly. It was like being inside a huge snow globe, she thought. Or maybe a music box. Everywhere she looked there were sparkling lights and Christmas trees. The air was filled with a rich, spicy, gingery smell. It was full of snow now too, the flakes twirling down lazily to settle on the cold pavements. Hannah had never seen anything so magical. She pulled up the furry hood of her parka round her neck and shivered happily.

"What do you think we should do first?" Mum asked, squeezing her hand. "I can't believe it's started to snow. It's just perfect!"

"I want to go on that, Mum!" Hannah's sister Olivia said, pointing at the huge Ferris wheel glittering above the square.

"It's so big!"

"But it's snowing!" Hannah pointed out.

"Actually, I think it's a great idea," Dad said. "That way we'll get to see all of the market and we'll know what there is to do. And it isn't snowing much, Hannah, just a few flakes. I don't think it'll stop us seeing the view."

Hannah nibbled her bottom lip doubtfully. The wheel really was very big. It was moving now, twirling slowly round, and the red-painted seats looked wobbly. She wasn't sure she wanted to be all the way up there. But Olivia was dancing about excitedly, desperate to dash across the square and join the queue. Olivia was two years younger than she was. If her little sister was brave enough to go on the wheel, Hannah wasn't going to admit she was scared.

She did sit huddled up close against Mum, though, when they finally got into the little carriage. Dad was sitting opposite, with his arm round Olivia's waist, holding on to her tight. She was so keen to see everything that she wanted to lean right out over the edge.

"Are you OK?" Mum whispered as the wheel gave a lurch and their carriage started to rise slowly in the air, swinging back and forth.

"Yes," Hannah squeaked. "It's just… It's just high."

"I know. I'm a bit nervous about it too. Olivia takes after your dad. He always wants to go on those big rides, doesn't he?"

Hannah nodded. It made her feel a bit
better that Mum was scared as well. Better
enough to lean sideways a little and peer
at the market below. She hadn't realized
how big it was until now. The huge square
was filled with hundreds of stalls and
sideshows, all lit up with glittering lights.
The *Striezelmarkt* was the biggest of the
Christmas markets in Dresden but there

were lots of others – they spread out all across the city. Since they were only there for a couple of days, Mum and Dad had said they should come to this market first, since it was the oldest – maybe even the first Christmas market there had ever been.

There had been a market here in the square since 1434, nearly six hundred years in the past. Of course, the city had changed a lot since then. Mum and Dad had explained that during the Second World War, the British had bombed Dresden very heavily and hardly any of the old buildings were left. It had made Hannah feel strange to hear that. She'd known about London being bombed in the war but she hadn't thought about the bombs her own country had dropped.

"Oh, there's a carousel," Hannah said,

pointing. She could just make out the horses galloping under the stripey roof. The carousel music threaded faintly through the air towards them, over the rattle of the wheel and the chattering crowd. "And there's a … I don't know what it is. There, look." They stared down at the glittering tower below. "Is it another carousel? There's figures on it but I can't see anyone riding on them, though."

Dad leaned over to look too. "Oh, I know this one! It's a Christmas pyramid." He scrunched up his nose, frowning. "Let me see if I can get this right. A *weihnachtspyramide*. They're very traditional. People here have been making them for years. They have a fan at the top – those blades, can you see? Like a ceiling fan. You light candles underneath.

Then when the hot air rises it makes the fan spin round. There's always a giant one at the Christmas market, though I think the candles on this one are electric. I read about it in the guide book."

"It's so pretty," Hannah said. "Can we go and look at it, Mum? The wheel's going back down now."

"We'll look at everything, don't worry!" Mum said, hugging her and laughing. "The tree, the giant advent calendar."

"The ice rink," Hannah's dad put in, and Olivia squeaked with excitement.

"Yes, yes! Can we go skating now?"

"Later on. There's a place close by where they have a huge Christmas tree right in the middle of the ice rink," Dad said. "Let's go and look at some of the stalls first and then we can see everything else. Maybe we could get some gingerbread?" He helped Hannah and Olivia off the metal steps and then sniffed loudly, making them laugh. "I can smell all those spices and I'm starting to feel hungry."

They wandered along the pathways between the wooden stalls. Each one was like a little hut and the shiny red roofs were slowly disappearing under a layer of snow. There was so much to look at that Hannah knew she'd never be able to see it all. She kept turning round to gaze up at the pyramid above them and the enormous Christmas tree, which was even taller than the Ferris wheel. Dad bought cups of hot chocolate and Hannah thought it was far nicer than any chocolate she'd had at home. There was a sweet, spicy taste to it – or maybe it was the snowflakes landing on the whipped cream top that made it so delicious.

Mum wanted to get some Christmas decorations, so she kept stopping to look at the stalls. But there were so many that Hannah didn't see how she was going to choose.

"Oh, look," Mum said, stopping at a display of brightly painted wooden figures. "We could have that Father Christmas one – he'd look lovely on the mantelpiece."

Hannah and Olivia were looking at the stall across the path, full of enormous, stripey lollipops. They both had a little bit of spending money and the lollipops looked like they might last a week, they were so huge.

"Dad, can you ask that lady how much the lollies are?" Hannah glanced back at her parents but they were busy discussing which of the Father Christmases had the nicest face and didn't hear her. "Hey, don't wander off!" She caught Olivia's sleeve. If her little sister went off on her own, they might never find her again. "We'll ask them again in a minute. Let's look at the figures. I think Mum's going to buy one."

Olivia muttered something grumpy about wanting a lollipop now but Hannah knew she wasn't really hungry. They were both full of hot chocolate and the rich spiced gingerbread Dad had bought.

"They're beautiful," Hannah breathed, coming to stand next to Mum. The stall was packed with shelves and shelves of shining figures. Elves, dancers, fairies, tin soldiers and the funniest little carved animals. Hannah smiled at one small cat that looked just like their tabby cat, Misty.

"Aren't they? It's so hard to decide. Some of them are puppets, girls, can you see? The ones hanging up there – they have strings."

Hannah nodded, peering up at the puppets dangling from the ceiling. There was a gorgeous angel puppet with silver wings but she couldn't read the price on the little paper ticket hanging from the angel's painted foot. She had a feeling that the puppets might be very expensive. No two were the same, and the painting was so delicate. She leaned sideways to look at the figure behind the angel. She couldn't quite tell what it was, but she thought it was an animal. It definitely had fur.

"You like it?" The elderly stallholder smiled at her. "You want to see?"

He turned round to grab a pole with a hook on one end, obviously made for fetching down the stringed puppets.

Hannah looked worriedly at Mum. What if the man thought she was going to buy the puppet? She was almost certain it would cost too much.

"It's all right," Mum said, patting her hand. "He's only being nice."

"Here..." The old man held up the puppet in front of Hannah, carefully straightening out the strings. "It's a little bear, you see?"

Hannah nodded, forgetting all about the price. The bear puppet was shiny with new paint but there was something about it that looked old. Hannah could imagine it in a museum, in a glass case. It wasn't a cuddly teddy bear sort of bear.

Although it was carved to be round and a bit podgy like a cub, it was a wild-looking creature, with shaggy brown-black fur and sharp teeth glinting in its muzzle.

Round its neck was a ruff made of red and white sparkly satin, like a clown's, but Hannah didn't think it suited the bear. It looked as if the cub would quite like to chew it off. Even with the silly ruff, the bear looked fierce. It had dark eyes that gleamed wickedly as if it wanted to leap off the counter and charge away into the market. Hannah could imagine the bear stealing sausages and gingerbread, sending the crowds squealing.

"Did you make it?" she whispered, looking up at the stallholder, and he nodded.

"Yes, yes. I make them all. Is nice?"

"Yes! *Very* nice." Hannah nodded enthusiastically.

"I make it dance for you," the old man told her, carefully positioning the wooden cross that held the strings. He set the bear's back paws on the counter and then began to twist his hand, cleverly bouncing the arms of the cross so the strings made the bear's paws tap and wave.

There had been music in the background the whole time they had been at the fair. Christmassy music floated across the square from a brass band and the different rides had bells playing jingly tunes. But all that seemed to fade away as the old man danced the bear across the counter for Hannah and a new sound started up. There was only a drum at first, a faint, insistent beat that seemed to get louder as the bear danced on. Then a flute, piping a sharp jig from somewhere close by. Hannah glanced round, thinking the player must be right behind her but there was no sign of anyone.

The music made the bear dance faster, Hannah thought, and then she smiled to herself. That didn't make sense – the bear was only a puppet and she knew it was the old man making him dance... But she could hardly see the strings now and the cub's hind paws were rattling hard on the counter. Its face twisted, the teeth showing more, its small, round ears flattening. The bear looked angry, almost scared, and the bouncy music made Hannah's heart thump sickeningly hard.

And then the old man stopped twisting the wooden cross and the bear was a puppet again, sagging on its strings.

Hannah blinked. There were tears in her eyes and she didn't know why.

"What happened?" she whispered, and Mum glanced down at her.

"Are you all right, Hannah? You look a bit pale."

"Um. Yeah… Did you hear that music? The drum?"

Mum shook her head. "No, only the music from the carousel. I wonder if we need to go back to the hotel? You look ever so tired."

"I'm not. It doesn't matter." Hannah gazed at the bear cub, biting her bottom lip. The stallholder had made the puppet sit, its hind paws stuck out straight in front, the strings coiled neatly beside it. Its pointed muzzle was different now, carved so it was almost smiling. The cub was such a handsome creature in its stripey ruff. There was nothing of the sad, angry bear from before.

"It dances nice," the old man said, smiling at Hannah, and she smiled back slowly. Had the old man seen what had happened? He must have done – he had been the one making the bear dance so strangely. But he didn't seem troubled. He tapped the bear's wooden head affectionately with a fingertip and chattered on. "It is good carving, I am very pleased. Nice paint. But perhaps you like something pretty instead? A little Christmas fairy?" He waved at the shelves behind him, the line of wooden dolls, and began to pick up the bear's strings, ready to hang it back up on the ceiling.

Hannah shook her head and reached out for the bear. But her fingers hovered over its paws – she didn't quite dare to touch it. "No! Please don't put it away. It's beautiful…" She tugged at Mum's coat sleeve and whispered, "Is it expensive? Have I got enough money?"

The old man smiled again and held up the ticket tied to the bear. Mum made a thoughtful "Mmmm" noise, and Dad shook his head.

"That's quite a bit, Hannah. It would be all the spending money we said you could have and a little more. Nothing left over for amazing lollipops." He waved at the stall behind them and Olivia danced up and down impatiently.

"Can we go and get a lolly now?"

"Special price, for the bear and the Father Christmas," the old man put in, scribbling something down on a pad and showing it to Mum.

"Well, maybe… Do you really want the puppet, Hannah? You haven't had a chance to see anything else yet! There are so many markets and it's our first day here."

"I really, really want it. The bear's special, Mum. Can't you see?" This time Hannah let herself touch the bear's wooden paw and just for a moment it felt like fur.

Chapter TWO

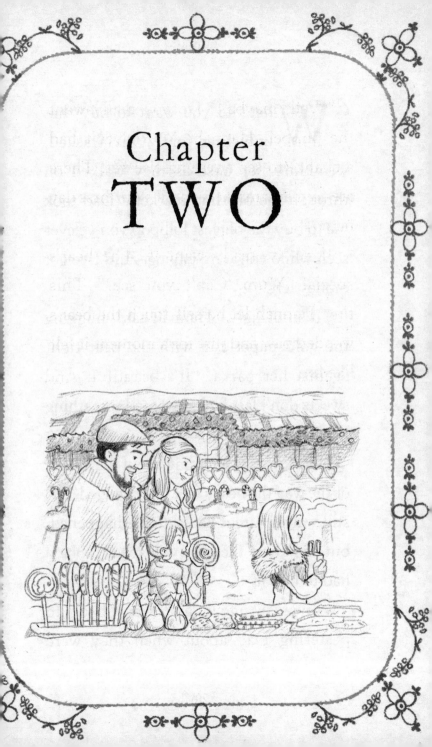

"What did you want to buy that ugly bear for?" Olivia asked, wrinkling her nose as they walked on through the bustling market. "Dad took me to buy the biggest lollipop you've ever seen while you were paying. *And* I've got money left."

"It's not ugly," Hannah said, hugging the gold paper bag with the bear tight against her parka. "It's beautiful. And sweets don't last long. I wanted something I can keep forever."

She didn't say anything about the music, or the way the bear's face had changed. She still wasn't sure it had actually happened, but she knew the bear was special. She'd had to buy it.

Olivia shrugged and went back to pestering Dad about when they were going to go ice skating.

"You haven't changed your mind?" Mum said, a little anxiously, and Hannah smiled at her.

"No. I love it. Can we go and look at the Christmas pyramid now? The puppet man had one on his stall, did you see? But it didn't have any candles in it."

Mum nodded. "Good idea."

They followed the brightly lit pathways between the stalls, peering up every so often at the pyramid towering above. It must have about six or seven layers, Hannah thought. Dad was right – it was meant to look as if it was powered by candles. Except the candles on this huge pyramid were electric ones, taller than Hannah.

Even Olivia went silent when they arrived in front of it. It was mesmerizing, standing there watching as the painted figures went slowly spinning past – soldiers in red uniforms, dancing fairies and a crowd of ice skaters in medieval-looking clothes. Hannah loved the top layer, which was all angels, playing long trumpets out into the crowd. There was a layer of animals too, with a bear quite like her puppet. She patted the bag lovingly and leaned against Mum's shoulder.

"It's starting to snow again," Mum said. "Maybe we should go back to the hotel and get some dinner? It's been a long day – we were up so early for the flight."

"But ice skating…" Olivia murmured, swallowing the end of her words in a yawn. "I suppose we could go tomorrow…"

"I promise," Dad told her. "Tomorrow's going to be amazing."

❄ ❄ ❄

Back at the hotel after dinner, Olivia's tiredness was making her even sillier and more annoying than usual. She wouldn't stop dancing about and bumping into things, and she kept jumping on Hannah's bed while she was trying to read her book.

"Get off," Hannah muttered. "We're meant to be going to sleep. You said you were tired!"

"I'm not tired now," Olivia sang, twirling round and round in her pyjamas. "I'm on a Christmas pyramid!"

"Just stop it!" Hannah snapped. "I'm going to clean my teeth. Get into bed!"

"Girls, you were supposed to be going to bed!" Mum called from the adjoining room, and Hannah glared at her little sister.

"See!"

Olivia slumped down on to the bed and stuck out her tongue. Hannah marched into the bathroom and shut the door hard.

She couldn't really hear Olivia from inside the bathroom but she seemed to have gone quiet. Perhaps she was nearly asleep, Hannah thought hopefully, sneaking the door open again.

She wasn't. She was sitting on Hannah's bed, the bag from the market stall on her lap, and she was dancing the bear puppet around on the bedspread. The strings were tangled up already.

"What are you doing?" Hannah gasped, staring at her sister in horror. "Did you take it out of the bag? Give it back! I never said you could play with it!" She lunged for the bear puppet, trying to snatch it out of Olivia's hands.

"I'm only looking!" Olivia wailed, not letting go.

"Give it to me!" Hannah pulled hard. There was a cracking, splitting noise and the bear's arm came off.

"You broke it!" Olivia whispered.

"My bear!" Hannah let the puppet drop on to the rumpled bedcover and stared at it. All that magic and strangeness – and it had gone. The bear cub was just a broken, splintered toy now.

"What on earth is going on?" Dad put his head round the connecting door between the rooms. Then he came right in and looked at them sternly. "What are you two arguing about? You're supposed to be asleep!"

Hannah handed him the bear, too upset to speak, and Dad turned it over in his hands with a sigh. "Broken already? I don't believe it, Hannah. You've only had it a couple of hours."

Hannah swallowed her tears, her voice shaking as she tried to speak. That just wasn't fair. "Olivia took it out of the bag! I never said she could play with it! I hadn't even unwrapped it!"

"I only wanted to see what was so special about it…" Olivia muttered. "You were the one who pulled it apart."

"Because you wouldn't give it back!" Hannah gulped tearfully, her shoulders heaving. The bear was ruined.

"I can mend it for you when we get back

home," Dad said, showing the pieces to Mum, who'd followed him into the room. "It should go back together with a bit of glue. Here, let's pack it away. Don't worry, Hannah, I'm sure we can sort it out." He took the pieces and wrapped them carefully in the tissue paper, slipping them into the gold paper bag.

"It won't be the same," Hannah whispered. She was too upset to be grateful. She took the bag, clutching it tightly. She couldn't stop crying. "It's all Olivia's fault. She spoils everything!"

"You two had better get into bed," Mum said, sounding cross. "We don't want to hear another word out of you."

Hannah put the bag on the little table, next to the lamp, and then got into bed. She rolled over so she was pressed close up against the wall, sniffing sadly. Why hadn't she just told Mum and Dad to make Olivia give the bear back? If only she hadn't grabbed it. *It was Olivia's fault*, she thought miserably. *Not mine.*

"Sorry, Hannah," she heard her sister whisper into the dark room.

Hannah didn't say anything.

She woke up later that night, still angry. There was a hard lump of fury blocking her throat and her eyes felt swollen from crying. It was cold, far colder than it had been when she went to bed. Hannah tried to reach for the duvet to pull it back round her shoulders but she couldn't find the edge. Maybe it had slipped off the bed? She sat up and started to pat around her in the darkness, feeling for the cover. But all she could feel was something rough, scratchy – almost spiky, like straw. A sick feeling stirred in her stomach. Was she even in the hotel room any more?

I couldn't have got out, she thought worriedly. *I don't think I could have undone the door…* She had once unlocked the front door at Gran and Grandad's house when she was sleepwalking, though. *I thought I'd stopped doing that. I haven't walked in my sleep for ages. Oh, where am I?*

Under the spiky stuff was a hard floor, Hannah realized, poking at it. Definitely not carpet, like the hotel room. She *was* somewhere else and it was very dark. She could hardly see anything, just shadowy shapes. Wherever she was didn't smell like the nice clean hotel room either. It smelled awful – a bit like when they drove past a field full of pigs back home. And it was so cold. Hannah huddled her arms round herself and shivered. Then her fingers clutched suddenly on her sleeve and all her breath seemed to disappear.

She had gone to bed in the new Christmassy pyjamas Mum had bought especially for their holiday – red with little white snowflakes all over. They were made of a fleecy fabric, thick and soft. She definitely wasn't wearing those now. The sleeve she held was rough, some sort of coarsely woven fabric. And instead of pyjama bottoms, she had on a skirt, a long, full skirt. She could feel it round her ankles. It wasn't like anything she owned, Hannah was sure.

She reached down and felt her feet.

They should have been bare but she was wearing shoes, an oddly shaped, clumpy sort of shoe that felt like leather, with buckles. Her eyes were starting to adjust to the darkness a little – and perhaps it was getting lighter too? She'd thought it was the middle of the night but could it really be near to dawn? She peered at the strange shoes and the heavy woollen skirt, then at the top she was wearing. It had buttons, she realized. Buttons to do up a little fitted jacket.

These *definitely* weren't her clothes, she thought, frowning to herself. They were old-fashioned clothes, like the ones that the figures on the puppet stall had been wearing. But why was she sitting on a dirt floor covered in straw, wearing someone else's old-fashioned outfit?

Hannah was still trying to work out what could possibly be going on when something stirred in the straw on the other side of the room. Something turned round, or maybe rolled over in its sleep. She was fairly certain it was a something, not a *someone*, because whatever it was made a grunting, growling noise that definitely wasn't a snore. It was an animal noise.

I suppose that explains the straw on the floor, Hannah told herself. She was in a stable. It was probably a horse.

But it didn't sound like a horse. Horses didn't growl. She edged a little further back, across the cold stone floor, and the rustles and growling on the other side of the stable were replaced by a thoughtful, listening silence.

Whatever it was knew she was there.

Half of Hannah wanted to huddle in the corner of the stable with her eyes closed and her arms over her head. The other half wanted to stay where she was, watching, poised to run. Though what if there wasn't anywhere to run *to*?

The braver half won, just about. She

peered through the shadows at the dark lump that wasn't a horse, trying to see what it could be. She could feel it staring back. It growled again, a deep, throaty noise, and Hannah swallowed hard, her heart thumping. That growl…

She'd never actually met a bear but she'd seen them on TV and the noise sounded very bear-like. How could she possibly be shut up in a stable with a *bear*?

Chapter
THREE

Hannah looked down at the floor hurriedly, thinking she shouldn't stare at the creature. The bear – if that's what it was – could probably see better than her in the dark and she really didn't want the growly animal to think she was dangerous. But at least it didn't seem to be planning to attack her right now.

It was shuffling around uncertainly in the straw and it didn't sound as if it was about to make a move. Maybe it was as frightened as she was? She would just have to wait until it was light enough to see properly and then she could make a run for it. Hopefully the bear wasn't between her and the stable door.

The light changed slowly. Hannah dug her fingernails into her palms, trying to stop herself shaking as the dark shape in the corner gradually became clearer and clearer.

It was hunched up in a pile of straw, sitting like a dog. Was that all it was – a big dog? But as Hannah peered forwards she saw the little, round ears, the thick heavy paws, its deep muzzle. The bear was watching her, letting out little, worried growls.

Small growls from a small bear, Hannah thought, almost laughing with relief. It was only a baby, a cub, round-faced and sweet like a teddy.

Hannah was starting to think that she didn't need to be scared after all when something else moved on the other side of the wall. The stable was divided up into stalls, she realized. She was in one stall and there were more on either side of her.

The stall had a door that opened into a passage – the kind of door that could be opened at the top so the horse could look out into the rest of the stable. The walls were made of wooden slats and didn't look very strong.

The wall shook as the creature next door lumbered to its feet and banged against it, and Hannah gasped out loud. There was a moment's silence and then a roar, so dark and deep and furious it seemed to shake the air. Hannah saw a glittering eye through the crack between the slats, then a flash of yellowish teeth.

The cub in the corner whimpered and Hannah squeaked with fear. She leaped to her feet, scattering straw, as the creature flung itself against the wall again. The wooden slats seemed to bulge inwards and

Hannah scrabbled frantically at the latch on the stall door. Whatever it was – another, bigger, bear? – it looked like it was trying to break in. She had to get out of here.

At last she fought the door open, remembering to slam it shut in case the cub came after her. She dashed out into the dirt-floored passage that ran along the front of the stalls. Light was coming in from a door at the end of the passage. In fact it was so much lighter now she was out of the stall that Hannah was half blinded. She didn't even see the boy hurrying the other way and crashed straight into him, going flying.

Hannah landed on the earthy floor with a yelp and lay there dazed for a moment while several horses put their heads curiously over the half doors.

"I'm so sorry! Are you hurt? Here, let me help you up." The boy set down the big lantern he was carrying so he could pull Hannah to her feet. Then he brushed bits of straw off her skirt, muttering that he hadn't meant to bump into her and was she really all right?

"It's fine…" Hannah kept saying. "I'm not hurt. I should be the one saying sorry.

It was me that ran into *you*..." Then, seeing him looking anxiously around, she added, "What's the matter? I'm not cross, please don't worry."

"It isn't that..." The boy grabbed the lantern again. "Look, can we talk about this outside, once we're safely away from here?"

Hannah hesitated for a moment. It wasn't like she wanted to stay in the stable. The huge creature in the next-door stall hadn't stopped growling. Plus the place smelled awful. But she still had no idea where she was. Wouldn't someone be coming to look for her? Surely Mum and Dad would notice she was missing soon.

"I'm not supposed to be here..." said the boy. He suddenly looked stricken.

"Are you staying at The Golden Ring? Please don't tell anyone you saw me!"

"No, I'm not..." Hannah said uncertainly. This definitely didn't look like part of their hotel. And the boy was wearing old-fashioned clothes too. Rather saggy brown leggings, with a tunic over the top, and a squashy hat. Where *was* she?

"You're not supposed to be here either? Then let's go!" The boy grabbed her hand and started to tow her along the passage to the door. Hannah went with him – she didn't know what else to do.

"They might have heard us," the boy hissed. He peered around the door, then darted out. "Hurry up!"

Who might have heard us? Hannah

wondered as they raced across the stone-flagged yard and out into a great square, overlooked by a tall church with a thin spire. The square seemed strangely familiar and in the half-light of the winter morning, she whirled past the old houses in confusion.

The square was already busy, even so early in the day. Carts and barrows stood everywhere, with people bustling all around. Tables were being set up on trestles and awnings built. It was a market, Hannah realized. Like the Christmas market she had been at the day before – but so different. The glittering lights had gone, replaced by a few smoky torches in brackets attached to the walls and a few lanterns with candles like the one the boy was holding.

This market was for business, Hannah
saw, as he hurried her along. It wasn't a
fun, holiday sort of place. All the stalls
seemed to be selling useful things like
carved wooden plates and dried herbs.
A man was wandering about selling hot
pies from a tray slung round his neck
but there were no food stalls frying up
sausages, or handing out mugs of hot
chocolate. And certainly no carousels or
Ferris wheels or Christmas pyramids. She
could smell gingerbread, though, as they
dashed past.

The boy ignored the market entirely.
He darted across the edge of the square,
and then in and out of narrow lanes and
alleys, with Hannah panting after him.

"Slow down!" she gasped. "I need to
stop a minute!"

"Not yet," he said. "We'd better get well out of the way. Don't want anyone remembering me hanging around."

Hannah was starting to wonder what exactly the boy had done to make him so nervous. Perhaps he was a pickpocket? That bustling market would be a perfect place to rob people. Maybe she shouldn't have followed him…

Just then, the boy came to a stop by a crumbling wall. "We should be safe here for a bit," he told Hannah. "Come on, duck down on the other side." He clambered over the wall and as Hannah climbed after him she saw they were just above the river. Mum had said they might go on a boat trip… She shook her head wearily and sat down next to him, leaning against the old stone wall.

"Not too busy along here yet," the boy explained, setting down the lantern. He opened its door – it wasn't glass, but some kind of murky yellowish stuff, set into a metal frame – and then he blew out the candle. "There. Are you really all right?" he asked, looking her up and down. "You took a terrible tumble. And you seem ... a bit dazed?"

Hannah felt like snapping back that he would too, if he'd suddenly found himself somewhere so strange and different, but she held her tongue. It didn't seem a very good idea to go telling him she didn't know where she was, or what was happening. Better to keep that quiet a little while longer. Especially since she was pretty sure the boy wouldn't believe her if she told him what she was beginning to think had happened.

That she'd gone to sleep and woken up hundreds of years before...

Hannah decided it was her turn to ask the questions. "What are you running away from?" she demanded. "And why were you in the stable in the first place? Did you steal something? Is that why you were so keen to get away?"

The boy drew back, frowning. "I could ask you the same thing!" he pointed out. "You said you weren't staying at The Golden Ring, so what were you doing in their stable? And right inside that stall! You weren't supposed to be there either!"

"I never said I was," Hannah retorted.

"So what were you doing there? Where did you come from?"

Hannah stared at him. It felt as if a great deep pit had opened up right in front of her feet and she was dithering on the edge. The fright of hearing that huge creature in the next-door stall had driven away the awfulness of finding herself in this strange place. Now the boy's sharp questions brought it all back and she found her eyes filling with tears.

She sniffed hard and rubbed the sleeve of the little jacket across her eyes. She had to tell someone, even if it was a bad idea. It was too frightening to keep it all to herself. She didn't have to mention the going back in time part.

"I don't know," she admitted. "I don't know *anything*..."

"Oh..." the boy groaned, his voice softening. "I knew you were hurt more than you said you were. You hit your head! My little brother fell out of a tree picking walnuts last autumn, and he was addled for a day and a half..." He patted her sleeve. "It'll come back. He's perfectly well now, I promise you."

What if she *had* banged her head? It was possible, Hannah supposed. Then this could all be a strange dream. Or ... or maybe it was the other way round? What if her memories of Mum and Dad and Olivia and the Christmas market weren't real, and she was meant to be here all along? She shuddered. No, she wasn't going to believe that. "Maybe," she whispered.

"Give it a day or two," he told her gently. "Everything will come back." He eyed her worriedly. "Look, I'll tell you why I was in the stables, shall I?"

"Yes." Hannah rubbed her eyes again and nodded. "What were you doing? Did you steal something? You wanted to get out of there so quickly…"

"I didn't actually steal anything," the boy explained. "I was going to but then I bumped into you and I gave up. I was afraid we'd have someone along any minute to see what the noise was."

"So what were you going to steal?" Hannah asked.

He glanced at her sideways. "A bear."

Chapter FOUR

Hannah stared at the boy for a few moments, then shook her head. "Why? And ... and *how*?" Then she giggled, because it was all too strange. "Did you just feel like stealing a bear? Actually ... I was wondering, why are the bears in the stable anyway? There were two of them, weren't there? A little one, and a –" she swallowed – "a really big one?"

The boy nodded. "Benno and Luna. Benno's the big one. Luna's only a cub. I don't know if the bear leaders have a name for her yet but that's what I call her. She's only a few months old. She's tiny," he added, clenching his fists and looking so fierce that Hannah flinched. "Sorry... It just makes me angry."

"But ... but why?"

"Because they stole her. They stole

Benno too, I expect. But it's too late to take him back now he's fully grown."

"Is that what you want to do? Take Luna back? Take her back where?" Hannah asked slowly.

"Look, I'd better explain." The boy stared down at his hands, twisting them together while he thought what to say.

"Start with your name," Hannah suggested. "You never told me your name. I'm Hannah."

"Oh! Yes. Matthias." He bowed to her, very seriously, and Hannah tried not to smile. "I don't live here in the city," he went on. "I come from one of the villages, outside in the Heath." He saw her looking uncertain, and added, "The forest just outside the city?"

Hannah nodded.

"I came here for the market. It's an important one – they always hold it just before Christmas. My father's a woodcutter but we make wooden toys too. We sit by the fire in the evenings and carve them."

"Like puppets," Hannah said slowly. That was important somehow.

"Yes, exactly. Puppets, or little figures that jump when you pull the strings. I made a horse and cart too – my father said I should ask a good price for it. The wheels turn and I made a harness out of some scraps of leather. So I'm here to sell the toys. It's the first year Mother and Father have let me come by myself – it's a long walk into the city. I told them I was old enough and Father didn't need to come. It's hard work for my mother looking after the little ones and the animals if he's away. But really I wanted to come alone so I could try and find the bears."

"You knew they were here?" Hannah asked, frowning.

"I hoped they would be. So many people come in from the villages for the market. The bear leaders wouldn't want to miss that, I thought. And I was right!" He pounded his fist into his palm. "I came to the town yesterday and it was easy to find them. Everyone was gossiping about the jugglers and the fire-eater and the bears. I reckoned I could sneak into the stables around dawn when the bear leaders were still asleep. But then I ran into you instead, didn't I?"

"I just don't understand," Hannah muttered. "How did you know about the bear leaders? And why do you want to take the bear cub off them?"

"Because I saw them steal her," Matthias said bitterly. "I saw them when I was out looking for mushrooms in the woods. I should have tried to stop them." His voice shook. "But I wasn't brave enough. They killed her mother, you know. They caught her in a trap so they could get Luna away from her."

Hannah gasped. "That's so cruel!"

Matthias nodded. "She'd never have let them take her otherwise. A mother bear would fight to the death for her cub. She adored Luna," he added sadly. "I watched them, you see. I like watching, I've seen all sorts of creatures. Deer. Boar. Even wolves! And lots of bears. I carve a great many toy bears and other creatures. I'm very good at making animals because I spend so much time looking at them."

He sighed. "This cub's mother had her den not so far from our cottage last winter. I saw them together when they first came out in the spring. They never came near us if we were chopping wood – they knew to stay away from the noise. But sometimes if I was out gathering mushrooms or herbs, or picking up kindling, then I'd see them. She played with her like my

71

mother plays with my littlest brother and sisters. I watched them splash about in the river. Sometimes if I was out at night, I'd see them. Dark bears stealing through the forest in the moonlight. That's when I named her. I didn't want to just keep calling her the cub in my head.

"Then the men came." Matthias shivered. "I didn't understand what they were planning to do, not until it was too late. I didn't do anything to save her! She tried to climb a tree to get away from the men but one of them went after her and dragged her down. She was so frightened."

"That's horrible," Hannah whispered. "But … I still don't understand why they did it. What do they want the bears for?"

"To dance, of course." Matthias stared at her. "Haven't you ever seen a dancing bear?"

Hannah shook her head. "Don't they like dancing?" she asked doubtfully. Hadn't Matthias just said they loved to play? But Matthias had also told her the bear leaders were cruel. Perhaps the dancing wasn't fun for the bears after all.

Matthias swallowed hard. "I can't believe you've never seen them," he said at last, shaking his head. "Lots of people like to watch dancing bears," he admitted. "The bear leaders make money out of it – they wouldn't bother if they didn't. But I hate it. The bears only dance because they're trained to. They don't enjoy the music or anything like that."

"But you said they liked to play," Hannah said. "How do you know they don't like dancing?"

"Because the bear leaders have to hurt

the bears to make them do it. They're not really dancing!" Matthias growled back. "They train them to dance on hot metal, Hannah! The bears lift their feet up because the burning metal hurts. The bear leaders play a drum while they're doing it and then every time the bear hears the drum after that, it thinks its feet are going to be hurt again, so it lifts them up and it looks like it's dancing about."

Hannah shook her head, her eyes wide and dark. "No… That can't be right," she whispered. "No one would do that. It's too awful."

"I've seen them," Matthias said miserably. "They stayed in the village close to us for a few weeks last summer. They'd only just captured Benno and they needed time to train him up. Lots of the children tried to watch them training the bear but the men always chased them away. But I really wanted to see what they were doing, so I hid in the hayloft of the barn they were using, before they came in one morning. I listened to them talk and I watched them hurting him."

"No wonder Benno's so angry," Hannah said. "And I think he hates people. When he heard me in the stall next to him, he sounded as if he wanted to knock down the wall to attack me."

"Wouldn't you hate people, if they'd treated you so badly?" Matthias pointed out. "If I could get Benno away as well,

I would, but I don't see how I can. He's so fierce. He's only scared of Jacob and Albert – they're the bear leaders." He looked pleadingly at Hannah. "Don't you see? I can't let them do that to Luna."

"No, of course not. So what are you going to do now? I'm sorry I messed everything up for you."

"It probably wouldn't have worked anyway." Matthias sighed. "It wasn't much of a plan. And I don't know what I can do, except to go back to the market and keep an eye on the inn and the bear leaders while I'm selling my toys. There might be some chance of getting to Luna, I suppose." But he sounded doubtful, Hannah thought.

"You're not giving up?" she asked him anxiously.

Matthias shrugged. "I don't *want* to! But I don't know how I can get her away."

"You can't give up. Please." Hannah put her hand on his. "You can't let those men hurt her. She's so little, and she's already lost her mother!"

Matthias nodded, squaring his shoulders. "You're right," he said determinedly. "I have to rescue her. Somehow…" He looked at Hannah thoughtfully. "What about you? What are you going to do?"

"I don't know." Hannah picked up a stone, and tossed it into the brownish waters of the river, where it sank with a *glop*. "I … I really don't know."

"You could come with me," Matthias suggested. "You'll remember everything soon – I'm sure you will. But until then I feel like I ought to look after you. Maybe you can help sell the toys."

"Where are they, anyway?" Hannah asked, suddenly realizing he didn't have a bag with him.

"Back at the hostel where I spent the night. It's not far from the market. We'll nip back there and pick them up, and then try and find a space near the inn to hawk them. I don't have a proper stall – I just lay them out on a blanket. So, are you coming?"

Hannah nodded.

What else could she do?

The toys were beautiful. Hannah hadn't really known what to expect but they were so delicately carved and painted she wanted to play with them herself. As the morning wore on, Matthias sold his horse and cart, and several little carved animals. No one seemed to want to buy the bear puppet that was Hannah's favourite, though. She loved the figure's brightly painted eyes and the detail of its fur and its tiny claws. There was something so familiar about the little bear and that strange sad look on its face.

They still hadn't seen the dancing bears but there were several other entertainers wandering around the market. A young man was playing an odd instrument a bit like a guitar, and singing, and there was another who could walk on his hands and twist himself into all sorts of impossible shapes. Hannah had been most impressed by the fire-eater. He started off by juggling flaming wooden brands, which was clever enough, but then he really did seem to be putting them into his mouth. Hannah couldn't work out how he was doing it. Surely it had to be a trick? She stared after him as he sauntered past the stalls, followed by a crowd of children.

"Look!" Matthias nudged her. "The bear leaders! They're coming out!"

Hannah looked up and felt a coldness

grip her stomach. There was Benno, the huge brown bear who had terrified her early that morning, eyeing her through the wall of the stable. He was so big that he rolled from side to side as he walked and he looked angry. *No wonder,* Hannah thought. *If those men hurt him the way Matthias said.* There was a metal ring in his nose with a rope through it and his leader, a tall, bald-headed man, held a wooden staff attached to the other end.

Behind Benno came another man, smaller, with a thick brown moustache. He was carrying a huddled armful of dark brown-black fur. The cub! Hannah craned forwards, trying to see her better. She could feel Matthias tense up beside her and his breathing quickened.

"The tall man is Jacob and the one carrying Luna's called Albert. Look how scared she is," he muttered. "I've got to get her away."

"Yes," Hannah whispered, watching as a little boy scurried after the two men and began to beat a lively rhythm on a drum. An older boy followed, playing on a wooden flute, and the eerie piping cut

through Hannah like a cold wind. She had
heard it before, she knew she had. The
bitter fury on Benno's face was familiar
too. Strange, confusing memories stirred
inside Hannah. It was the puppet from
the Christmas market that had brought
her here, she remembered it now.

She could see Benno had heard the music
before as well – a shudder passed through

him, rippling his dull brown fur. He heaved himself on to his hind legs and a gasp ran through the gathering crowd. He was at least half as tall again as the man holding the staff. As he lumbered about waving his front paws, he was an awful mixture, terrifying and sad, both at the same time.

Maybe that was what made the dancing bears so popular – the sight of something so huge and grand and powerful doing a silly little dance. The crowd was loving it, cheering and laughing as the poor bear waltzed about, but the dance made Hannah want to scream. She wanted to yell in their faces to make them see how unhappy the poor bear was.

"I hate it," she hissed, her hands clenched into fists so tightly her nails bit into her skin.

"I know, me too." Matthias had tears in his eyes, she realized, and she patted his arm clumsily.

"At least we can get Luna away from those horrible people," she said quietly. "Or we can try…"

"We?" He looked at her in surprise.

"I'm going to help," Hannah told him firmly. "I have to, now that I've watched them. And I've never even seen a bear in the wild. All this must be so much worse for you, when you know how they should be."

This is why I'm here, she thought suddenly. *It's all because of the bears. That puppet I bought, it's a part of the story – it has to be. It's a sign.*

"I'm going to help," she said again, pushing away the memory of Dad holding the broken puppet. She couldn't think about her family, not now. "So, what can I do?"

"I don't know about this." Matthias shook his head. "We have to find where you belong. I was thinking perhaps you were a runaway, or an orphan. Your clothes are a bit tattered," he added apologetically.

"It sounds like I don't belong anywhere then," Hannah pointed out. "So I can definitely be part of the rescue."

Matthias still looked doubtful. "I can't go dragging you into this. What if you get hurt again?"

"I don't think I will," Hannah said slowly. "It seems as though I was meant to be here. Do you see what I mean? I think I'm supposed to help you save Luna."

Matthias eyed her worriedly and

Hannah sighed. She could tell he was thinking she'd banged her head very hard.

"Never mind about me," she said quickly. "We haven't any idea where I belong so I might as well be useful. I could be a lookout, couldn't I? You were worried about the bear leaders coming into the stables this morning. I could watch out for them while you get Luna."

"I suppose you could hang about the inn." Matthias gave a thoughtful look, studying her clothes. "If you made yourself look a bit more ragged – put some dirt on your face maybe – you could lurk around the inn yard and pretend to beg from the customers. That way you could keep an eye on the bear leaders. Just look at all the takings they're getting." He nudged her, nodding at the little boy who was now going around with a hat, collecting coins. "They'll be celebrating in the inn tonight, for sure."

"Yes! And I can tell you when they're busy drinking so you can slip in and rescue Luna!" Hannah hissed excitedly. "We can get her away from here, I know we can!"

Chapter
FIVE

It was much harder than Hannah had expected, begging in the inn yard. No one seemed very interested in giving her money. Several people shouted at her to get out of the way – mostly those who were more grandly dressed, she noticed. One man with a beautiful horse and a rich, fur-lined cloak even tried to kick her. But she *was* able to watch the bear leaders quite easily, since no one seemed to see a beggar child.

She saw the bear leaders come out several times with Benno and Luna, setting Benno dancing and walking around the crowd with the cub, showing her to the children. Luna had a collar on now, Hannah noticed, a red one like a clown's ruff. It had tiny bells on it, so she jingled whenever she moved. Although she didn't move much. She seemed stiff with fear, or maybe sadness.

Between performances, Hannah tried her best to look hungry and desperate. As the day went on, it got easier and easier. She *was* hungry. She'd had nothing to eat since last night. She kept seeing that man selling meat pies from a tray and the smell was making her feel almost dizzy. After the midday meal had been served at the inn, one of the kitchen girls took pity on Hannah and gave her a bit of old bread. It was stale and rather hard but she thought it tasted wonderful. It didn't fill her up much, though.

As well as being hungry, Hannah was cold, even though her clothes were made of thick fabric. There was snow piled heavily on the roofs above her and swept into dirty heaps in the inn yard, and the sky was a heavy yellowish-grey. It looked like it was about to snow again and the air felt freezing. Her hands had gone scarlet after an hour or so waiting about outside, and now her fingers were mauvish-white and they ached.

But she had found out something useful. She'd seen the bear leaders shutting the two bears away in the stalls. Then, spying round the door of the stables, she noticed they must be using the hayloft above as their room. They stumbled up a ladder, grumbling to each other and complaining to the boy with the drum that he hadn't been quick enough taking round the hat. Half the crowd had sloped off before he could get any money from them.

She'd have to let Matthias know how

close the men were to the two bears. They were lucky the bear leaders hadn't come down that morning when Benno had been throwing himself at the wooden wall. Perhaps they were used to him getting angry. Matthias was right, Hannah thought, it would definitely be better to steal Luna when the bear leaders were in the inn itself tonight. It was far too risky to try when they were only a ladder's length away.

"Did you tie that latch shut?" someone growled up above, and Hannah flinched.

"Course I did!"

"You'd better be sure, Albert. You know what Benno's like – he's crafty. We don't want him getting out again."

"I told you, I tied it up tight!" Albert snapped, and Hannah shivered, imagining

Benno loose and running around the marketplace.

She and Matthias had agreed to meet up again in the early evening so she could let him know if she'd found out anything useful. When the bear leaders came down for their next show, Hannah followed them. She sneaked behind the little parade over to Matthias, who was putting the last few wooden toys into a big pack.

"We have to be careful. They all sleep in the loft above the stable," she murmured, tucking her hands up inside her armpits. It was colder than ever and she could hardly feel her fingers. "I think this is the final time they're bringing the bears out. I heard Jacob say that Benno's in a temper. They won't risk it again. They've done well with the takings, though."

"Watch out, boy." The man selling the meat pies eyed Hannah suspiciously as he wandered past. "Don't let that one pinch your purse. She's been hanging around the inn yard all day. She'll have your coins as soon as look at you!"

Hannah glared at him. How dare he? Yes, she'd been begging, although all she'd actually got was a bit of old bread, but she definitely hadn't stolen anything. She was about to say so when she remembered they were trying not to get themselves noticed, and she bit her lip hard to stop herself snapping at the pieman.

Instead she hung her head and scuttled away back to the yard. Through the open stable door, she watched the bear leaders shutting the bears back in their stalls and putting down their food. Then all four, the two men and the boys, trooped out of the stable and across to the inn. The little drummer boy was whining and pulling at Jacob's sleeve. "Can't I have a proper plate of stew? I'm starving. I only got a bit of bread and cheese last night..."

Hannah gave them a little while to get

settled, then she hurried to the back door, looking hopefully at the kitchen girl who'd given her the bread early on. She hadn't eaten anything all day except that bread and she was so hungry.

"No, no, off with you!" the girl muttered, hurrying to the door. "You'll get me in trouble, you will."

Hannah felt her eyes brighten with tears. She was so hungry. She looked pleadingly at the girl.

"Oh, go on then, here. You'll freeze if you don't have something inside you." She glanced behind her and saw the cook had her back to them, stirring something over the fire. "She'll have my hide if she's counted these, now get out of here!" She grabbed a pasty off the big wooden table, stuffed it into Hannah's hand and pushed her out of the door.

"Thank you!" Hannah whispered. The pasty smelled strange and delicious – it seemed to be filled with some sort of heavily spiced meat. It was warm too and Hannah cradled it for a few moments, letting it thaw her numb fingers. She started to nibble it as she peered round the door to the main room of the inn, looking for Albert, Jacob and the boys.

Yes, there they were, sitting close by the fire. All four of them had big earthenware tankards and they looked as though they were planning to be there for a while. The pasty had warmed Hannah's frozen fingers a little but it was hard to look at the cosy room, with its great fire. She could scarcely feel her feet now.

Hannah looked down at her pasty – there was about half left – and reluctantly stopped eating. They might need to coax Luna to come with them and she wasn't sure if Matthias had eaten anything either. She darted out of the inn yard and into the square, peering around in the flickering light of the torches.

"Psst, I'm here."

She swung round and saw Matthias waving at her from the side of a stall.

"They're all in the inn. They had plates of food and they were drinking out of those big jars." She made a face. "Actually, I think the one with the moustache— "

"Albert. The other's one Jacob," Matthias put in.

"Yes, Albert. Well, him and the older boy who plays the flute, they were drinking a *lot*. He had a stone bottle he kept passing round and he'd gone all red. When I left, the flute boy was trying to sing and people were telling him to shut up. I think they'll be there for a bit, anyway. We should do it now. Here, I saved this – it's a meat pasty. In case you need to tempt Luna to go with you."

Matthias nodded and took the pasty. "Good idea. Come on then. You stay outside the door and keep watch."

"What shall I do if they come?" Hannah whispered worriedly. "I can't just yell or they'll know someone's there…"

Matthias nodded, frowning. "I hadn't thought of that."

"I could make a horse noise," Hannah suggested. She tried to whinny but it came out as a bit of squeak and she saw Matthias smirk. "Well, you think of something then!"

"Here." Matthias pulled a little round piece of wood out of his pocket. "I was working on this while I was waiting for people to buy my toys. It's a bird caller. You twist this bit, see. It sounds like a robin." He showed Hannah how to turn the end piece inside the whistle and a high chirruping sound floated out – so real that Hannah almost turned to look for the bird making it. "You try."

Hannah twisted the wooden toy and smiled to herself as she heard the robin chirp. "All right. Just make sure you're listening for it."

Together they crept across the yard, keeping close against the wall and watching for the stable boys. There were several horses in the other stalls now and Hannah wondered what they thought of the bears. Matthias slipped inside and she stood by the door, her heart thumping uncomfortably hard. She could hear a click as Matthias unlatched Luna's stall followed by a creak as he opened the door.

Then Hannah's thumping heart seemed to drop down inside her. There was a commotion going on over at the inn, perhaps a fight. She could hear yelling and a heavy thud as if someone had fallen. There were figures spilling out of the door and Hannah saw the landlord in his long apron shoving someone along in front of him.

"Not having you in here stirring up trouble!" he roared. "I don't care how much money you've got. You can all get yourselves back to the stables."

Her fingers fumbling, Hannah pulled at the bird whistle but the chirruping hardly sounded over all the shouting in the yard. It was too late, anyway…

"Matthias!" Hannah yelped, leaning in the door. "They're coming! The innkeeper kicked them out! Oh no…" She could see Matthias coming towards her, his face a pale blur in the dark stable, a squirming mass of small bear in his arms.

Hannah looked around desperately,

wondering what to do. The bear leaders were heading her way, their voices angry. Any moment now they were going to catch Matthias right in the middle of stealing their precious bear cub.

"The bear!" Hannah screamed. "Help! Help me! The big bear's loose!" She ran across the yard, yelling as loud as she could. "Oh, help me, he's after me!" She was banking on it being too dark for them to see she was making it up.

"What? The bear?" she heard Jacob growl. "Benno's loose? Albert, you fool, didn't I tell you to check you'd tied the latch shut?"

"I did!" Albert roared back. "Crafty old thing must have clawed it open somehow. We'd better get after him."

They hurried across the yard towards Hannah and she went on screaming. "He knocked me over," she wailed. "He ran out into the market! Oh, he nearly ate me!"

"Which way, girl?" Jacob, the tall one, grabbed her arm and shook her. "Stop that racket! Which way did he go?"

"In among the stalls," Hannah gasped out. "There, he's there, I just saw him!" She pointed wildly into the mass of shadowy market stalls and they charged off, Jacob racing ahead and Albert and the flute boy stumbling behind him. Hannah stared after them for a moment, hardly daring to believe it had worked. Perhaps Benno *had* escaped before…

"That was clever," Matthias whispered, coming up beside her. "We'd better get out of here."

Hannah felt like hugging him, except she wasn't sure about hugging a bear cub too. It had worked!

And then a figure loomed up out of the darkness with a burning torch. In the flickering yellow light, Hannah recognized the boy who played the drum.

Only three figures had lumbered away after the imaginary bear, Hannah realized now. She had been so delighted with the success of her trick, she hadn't understood what that meant.

"What you got there?" he demanded.

Hannah and Matthias stared at him dumbly. All the boy had to do was yell and the others would come racing back. Hannah could hear them blundering about in a side alley somewhere.

"You nicked the cub!" the boy breathed, staring at Matthias, his eyes widening.

"Yeah, and ... and we're not letting you have him back!" Matthias said, but Hannah could hear his voice shaking.

The boy said nothing and Hannah leaned forwards a little, watching his eyes in the torchlight. He wasn't looking at her, or Matthias. He was looking at the cub.

"We're taking her away, before those men can hurt her," she said softly. "She's scared."

"Get out of here," the boy snarled, waving his torch at them. "Go on!"

Matthias gaped but Hannah seized his arm and dragged him out of the inn yard. She was almost sure she heard the boy whisper something as they dashed away.

"*Look after her.*"

"I can't believe he let us go," Matthias hissed as they scurried along the side of the market place.

"Me neither. Which way are we going?"

"Towards the river again. Can you stand my pack up? It's just inside the alley there, look."

Hannah grabbed the pack. It had straps, a bit like her backpack for school, but it seemed to be mostly made of sacking.

"Shh! Here, have a bit of this," Matthias was murmuring to the bear cub. "Yes, that's good, isn't it? In you go – you eat it all up." He folded the top bit of sacking over the cub, who was greedily snuffling at Hannah's pasty. "Now, help me put it on." He crouched down and pulled one of the straps over his arm, and Hannah half lifted the pack so he could wriggle into the other one. "Oooof, she's heavy. Come on. Let's go."

"Are we crossing the river?" Hannah whispered. She could still hear the bear leaders charging about among the stalls, shouting at each other. The sooner she and Matthias were gone, the better. She didn't know when the men might go back to the stables and discover Benno had been there all along.

"Yes, over the bridge out of the city," Matthias said, heaving the pack higher on his back. "We should be able to get out of the gates before they shut them for the night. We need to cross the river and head along the bank for a while, then we take a path through the Heath. Come on." He darted into an alleyway and Hannah scurried after him. "Look for the castle – you'll see the tall spire. The gates and the bridge are close by."

"I can't see anything. It's too dark!" Hannah panted. "Do you know where you're going?"

"Sort of," he said. "Just … just look for the pointy towers. Yes, here! This is the main street, the Elbgasse!" Matthias grabbed Hannah's arm and dragged her into the wider street. "I can see the castle lit up at the end, we're not far."

Hannah peered forwards. She could hardly see anything – the dark bulk of a building, maybe? There were so few lights. "What time do they shut the gates?" she asked anxiously.

"At dusk. But it'll be later tonight because of the market. I'm sure it will…"

"It'd better be…" Hannah said, digging her nails into her palms and scurrying along. It was well past dusk, full dark already. "Can you go any faster?"

"She's heavy," Matthias panted. "I didn't think she'd be so heavy… Oh no!" he yelped as a sharp trumpeting sound rang out close by. There was a worried whimper from inside his pack. "They're about to shut the gates. Run!"

Hannah could just see it now – a tall white stone building, with a heavy arched gateway. There were people bustling around holding torches, obviously about to close the great wooden gates.

"Oh, please wait!" she gasped as they raced down the street. "Wait for us!"

"You two are cutting it fine," one of the guards growled as they flung themselves at the gates. "Are you setting off across the bridge now? It's dark!"

"Our father's waiting for us," Matthias told him, in between wheezing breaths. "Just over the bridge."

"We were supposed to meet him ages ago," Hannah put in. "But we got lost. He's going to be so cross with us!"

"Oh, very well then," the guard grumbled. "Out you go. Come on, I haven't got all night."

They hurried through, out on to the bridge, and Hannah turned back to watch the great gates groan shut behind them.

"We're out!" Matthias said. He sounded surprised, as though he hadn't thought they'd make it.

Hannah nodded. "But you know what's even better?" she said, hearing the thud of the bars dropping down to secure the gate. "Albert and Jacob – they're still inside. You did it! You got Luna away!"

"*We* did it." Matthias slung an arm round her shoulders. "You sent them on that wild goose chase among the market stalls." He chuckled to himself. "They'll probably run round the market hunting for Benno all night!"

Chapter
SIX

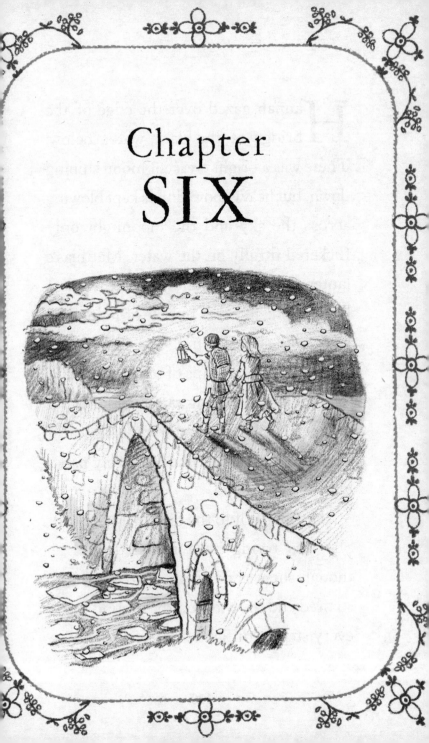

Hannah gazed over the edge of the bridge at the dark water below. There was a bright crescent moon shining down, but heavy snow clouds kept blowing across the sky and the moonlight only flickered fitfully on the water. Matthias's lantern cast a dull yellow gleam – it was like walking in a tiny bubble of light. The river was still flowing, just about, but there were great lumps of ice in the water. The night was getting rapidly colder and Hannah wished she had something warm to wear – something like her lovely parka with its furry hood.

"How far is it to the forest?" she asked. She was trying hard not to sound as though she was complaining but she was so tired and the snow on the ground made every step so difficult. Her feet felt twice as big as usual, all clumped with snow.

"Only about two hours but it's starting to snow again," Matthias said worriedly, putting out his hand to catch a crystal flake. He didn't have gloves either but he didn't seem to mind so much. "We're all right for a little while, since we only have to follow the river, but if it comes down heavily we'll have to stop. We can't risk missing our path."

Hannah nodded wearily. She didn't know whether to hope for it to snow or not. She was longing for a rest and something to eat but she kept trudging on. Matthias was walking just as far as she was *and* he was carrying a bear cub on his back.

She peered through the snow at the pack, wondering how Luna was. She must have finished the pasty ages ago. She'd expected the cub to try and claw her way out, or at least to make a fuss about being shut up. But there was no noise from inside. The little bear wasn't even wriggling. The quiet snow had wrapped them all up, muffling everything.

"It's no good," Matthias said, about half an hour later. "We have to stop. I can't see my hand in front of my face. There's no chance of finding the path on to the Heath now. We'll rest for a bit and wait for the snow to ease off."

"There's a boat over there," Hannah suggested. "I think..." she added doubtfully. It was hard to see through the snow. The boat was just a dark lump in the whiteness. It had been turned almost upside down on the bank of the river, to keep it from filling up with snow, she guessed. There was a line of darkness along the ground where the boat was propped up by the … well, she didn't know what they were called, the pointy ends. They could dig out the snow around it and wriggle underneath.

"Ah, perfect," Matthias said, clapping his hands together. Hannah helped him to lift off the pack. "I'm so glad you spotted it. I was thinking we'd just have to crouch under a tree or something."

It was amazing how much difference it made, being out of the snow. They were still huddled on the cold ground but at least there was a little shelter. The biting wind whistled round the sides of the boat and left them in a precious pocket of stillness. Hannah blew on her hands and tried not to whimper as the feeling began to come back.

"Shall we get her out?" she suggested. "Poor little Luna. I shouldn't think she likes being shut up in there." Then she hesitated. "If it's safe, I mean."

Matthias snorted. "I don't know if it's safe or not. It shouldn't be – she's a wild bear. But she's so scared of Albert and Jacob, she isn't behaving like a wild creature now. She's too terrified even to snarl."

He was undoing the straps of the pack

while he talked, folding back the heavy fabric and looking inside at the bear cub. Hannah saw Luna's black eyes glitter in the faint light of the lantern then the cub turned her head away, burrowing back into the pack. It was small and dark and safe in there, Hannah supposed. Luna didn't know who they were. She didn't know they were trying to take her home.

"Let's leave her," she said quickly to Matthias, who looked like he was about to try and grab the cub. "She's scared. Let her come out slowly."

Matthias nodded. "I suppose so. I wanted to take that collar off. It makes me feel so angry, seeing her dressed up like that." He glanced at Hannah. "Are you all right?"

"Just cold," she said, her teeth chattering.

"I haven't even got a blanket, or a cloak," Matthias said worriedly, peering at her in the lamplight. "You're so pale."

"I'll warm up soon. It's better in here out of the wind." Then she gave a little jump and a squeak. A damp nose had just dabbed against her wrist. "Luna," she whispered. "She came out by herself!"

The cub eyed Hannah for a moment, and then nudged firmly at her knees. Hannah had been huddled over, with her knees drawn up to her chin. Now she sat up, clumsily cross-legged in the heavy, damp skirt, and Luna lumbered into her lap. Then the bear cub curled up like a cat, like Hannah's own Misty. She even stomped round and round to get comfy, just like Misty did.

"She likes you," Matthias said, and Hannah thought he sounded a little jealous.

"Move the pack," she told him. "Come and sit closer. She can lie on both of us. Oh, Matthias, she's so warm. She's like a hot-water bottle."

"A what?" Matthias said, but he didn't really seem to be listening. He shuffled up next to her, looking hopefully at the bear cub. The little creature sighed heavily and sat up again. Then she slumped across both their knees, her head on Matthias's lap.

"I'm going to take this off," Matthias whispered, digging his fingers underneath the clown ruff collar. "I can't stand seeing her in it."

Luna peered round to see what was happening but she didn't wriggle. When the collar was unbuckled, she shook herself as if she was shaking off the feel of it round her neck. Her fur stood up all over in little damp prickles and she sighed again.

"I think she's going to sleep," Hannah said.

"We mustn't, though," Matthias warned her. "It's too cold – it's dangerous. And as soon as the snow stops, we have to go on." He rolled his shoulders and grunted. "I don't know how much longer I can carry her. She's a lot heavier than I thought she would be."

Hannah nodded. She knew Matthias was right and they mustn't sleep but Luna's blissful warmth was soaking through her and she was so, so tired. *Keep talking*, she told herself. *Keep awake.*

"What are you going to do with Luna once we get to the right place in the woods?" she murmured. "Will it be all right to leave her there? Isn't she a bit young to fend for herself?"

Matthias nodded. "She's definitely too young. I'm going to have to look after her until she's bigger. There's a fallen tree on the edge of the village. I thought it would make a good den."

"What about food?" Hannah asked.

"She won't be able to hunt…" Matthias admitted. "I don't think so, anyway. She's too small and she needs her mother to teach her. I watched a mother bear last year – she was teaching her cubs to fish in the stream. It was so funny! They got soaked and they kept splashing… But their mother just went on showing them. That's how it works." He sighed. "I can't teach her that. I'm not sure she'll ever learn to be a proper bear."

"You can't look after her for the rest of her life!" Hannah said. "And how are you going to find all her food?" She had a feeling Matthias's family didn't have a lot of money to live on. His clothes were patched and worn, and his boots had been mended over and over again.

"I don't know," Matthias said quietly. "But anything's got to be better than staying with Jacob and Albert. Hasn't it?"

Hannah nodded fiercely. "Of course! I wasn't saying that." She was silent for a moment, thinking. At last she said, "What she needs is a mother."

"I know." Matthias sighed.

"Well, can't we find her one?"

Matthias looked up, blinking. "What?"

"A bear who wouldn't mind another cub, maybe? I heard about farmers persuading sheep whose lambs had died to care for orphan lambs. Would that work for bears?"

Matthias sat up so quickly he almost hit his head on the floor of the boat. "There is a bear who's lost her cub! I've seen her! She comes to the river sometimes. She had a cub back in the spring too but the cub didn't seem to grow and it was very thin. It died a few weeks ago and since then she's been wandering the woods looking lost." He scowled, chewing his lip. "We'll just have to convince her to take Luna instead."

"Except she's a wild bear," Hannah said, wondering if her idea was silly after all. "I mean, how do we *convince* her to do anything? It probably isn't safe for us to go near her, is it?"

"Um, no," Matthias admitted. "No, most likely she'll be even less friendly than usual, because she's lost her baby. But maybe seeing Luna would distract her."

"So she could eat us?"

Matthias rolled his eyes. "Bears hardly ever attack people. Though a mother bear might, if you tried to hurt her cubs. That's why the bear leaders had to trap Luna's mother. But mostly they hunt small prey like mice. I've watched them eating moths and lifting up tree bark to find beetles! And they like fruit and mushrooms and honey. They hardly ever hunt anything big, like us. Besides, it's the winter – she'll be sleepy and slow. She ought to be curled up in her den but I think losing her cub confused her."

Hannah looked down at Luna, stretched across their laps, snoring a little. "Should she be hibernating too?" she asked. "Sleeping all winter, I mean," she added as Matthias looked confused.

"If she had a mother, she would be. But now I suppose she won't know what to do."

Hannah nodded. "If we want Luna to survive the winter, we definitely need to find a mother to teach her." She looked over at Matthias. "You'd better be right about them eating moths and things. If that bear eats us, I'm blaming you!"

Chapter
SEVEN

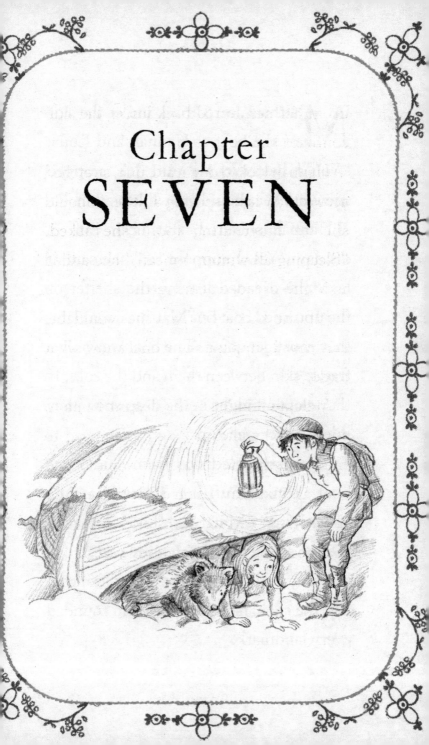

Matthias peered back under the side of the boat at Hannah and Luna. "You'd better come out. It's stopped snowing. We should go, while we can."

Hannah shivered, staring at him in dismay. "Yes, I suppose so," she said at last. She dreaded leaving the shelter of the upturned boat but Matthias was right, they must get going. The boat was only a fragile skin between them and the cold. If they slept all night in the deep snow they might never wake up.

They struggled out from under the boat, Luna snuffling sleepily at the snowdrifts. Matthias had replaced the candle in his lantern with a fresh one but they still couldn't see very far ahead, and the snow had smoothed and rounded every landmark.

"How will you know when we're there?"
she asked anxiously.

Matthias shrugged. "We'll see the trees.
It's spotting the path to the village that's
difficult. There's one huge fir tree where
the path starts."

Hannah looked around doubtfully.
There were trees along the bank of the
river too – looking for one particular fir tree
didn't sound as though it would be easy.
But Matthias had done this journey lots of
times, she supposed.

Matthias opened up his pack again and
looked at Luna, who was scuffling curiously
at the snow. It looked like she'd never played
in it before, Hannah thought. She couldn't
imagine Jacob and Albert giving the cub
a chance to explore. "Perhaps Luna could
walk?" she suggested. "You said how heavy

she was. Look, she likes the snow. We should let her walk instead of carrying her."

"Do you think she'll stay with us?" Matthias asked doubtfully. "What if she runs off? She doesn't really know us…"

Hannah took a few steps forwards, and called, "Here, little one. Little bear. Luna. Come on."

The bear cub looked up at the sound of her voice, and then glanced curiously at Matthias. Then she galumphed through the soft snow towards Hannah. Hannah laughed with delight. "She will! She likes us, Matthias. You call her, go on."

"Come, bear…" Matthias tried.

Luna stomped across to him and stood up on her hind feet, her front paws firmly planted on Matthias's knees. She nuzzled at his leggings and then jumped down and trotted off ahead of the children, looking back at them like a dog eager to set off on a walk.

"You see!" Hannah said. "She thinks she belongs to us." But then she wished she hadn't said it. They wanted the tiny bear to be free... She walked on hurriedly, stumbling in the snow.

The trees were starting to grow thicker as they shuffled along. Hannah's feet were stinging and burning with the cold now, her woollen stockings soaked. She envied Luna her thick fur and sharp claws – the cub didn't slip and slide around on the snow like she did. But she was starting to look tired. She probably hadn't had much chance to be outside for the last few weeks. This would be the furthest she'd walked in ages. Perhaps ever.

"There!" Matthias called, looking back at them. "There's the tree! Now we follow this path back to my village – it's just on the edge of the forest. But we'll need to go on a bit further and see if we can find the bear."

Hannah nodded eagerly but deep down she was wondering how easy it would be to find one bear in a huge forest... Still, at least they'd found the path.

Luna scampered on ahead with Matthias, sniffing at the trees excitedly and scuffling in the snowdrifts. She was like a little child out to play in the snow for the first time. Hannah was sure she knew this was where she belonged – she kept skittering across the path, delighted by each new smell. The bear was so funny and happy, Hannah forgot how cold and tired she felt. She had wondered if Luna would disappear off into the forest as soon as they were deep among the trees, but the cub seemed happy to stay with them. They had fed her, she supposed, and taken off her hated collar. The cub knew they were good.

"There's a light!" she burst out, a few minutes later. "Over there, through the trees." She pointed at the golden glimmer and Matthias nodded, looking relieved.

"That's the village – our cottage is on the far side of it." He lifted the lantern and looked at Luna, who was standing on her hind paws, sniffing curiously at the bark of a silver birch tree. "I suppose we'd better stay in the trees. We can't walk through the village with a bear cub, in case anyone sees us."

Hannah nodded her head. Though she

wished they could stay for a while – she longed to knock on the door of one of those comfortable little wooden cabins. To go in and get warm, perhaps drink some hot soup. Walking away from those bright lights seemed terribly hard. But Matthias was right.

"Come on, little one," she called to Luna, and reluctantly the bear cub left the tree and trudged towards her. She looked weary now too, Hannah thought. Her head was drooping and her paws dragged in the snow. But she followed Matthias and Hannah as they set off deeper into the woods, the lantern lighting up the black tree trunks as it swung by.

"What are you looking for?" Hannah asked Matthias, stamping her feet a little as he peered at the snowy path. "Tracks?"

He nodded. "Yes, but with all the snow we had earlier on, I'll be lucky to find any. We'll just have to try the places I've seen the bear before and hope." He made a face. "She might even have gone into her den for the winter by now. I don't know what we'll do then…"

"Don't say that," Hannah said. "We have to find her. Look at Luna."

The cub was pressed up close by her, leaning against her leg. She looked almost asleep.

"Maybe I should put her in the pack again," Matthias said worriedly.

"She's exhausted." Then he sighed. "And so are you. We could be hours, trying to find the bear. You and the cub had better wait here."

Hannah wasn't sure about being left behind. But if she didn't stay, Matthias would have to carry Luna again and he was worn out already. She swallowed. "Is there anywhere to shelter?"

Matthias lifted the lantern high, glancing around, and then he smiled. "Yes! I know the perfect place. Come on! It isn't far, I promise." He set off along the path and then turned by a patch of holly, shiny-dark and studded with red berries. "Along here, there's a fallen tree – the one I was thinking Luna could have for a den. Yes, there."

All Hannah could see was a long,

domed hump in the snow but Matthias seemed quite certain. He handed her the lantern and started to dig and kick at the snow. "It's rotting away and it's quite hollow inside – I crawled in it once to see. It's definitely big enough for you and Luna to curl up for a while."

Beetles, Hannah thought. *And spiders and mould and mushrooms.* She closed her eyes for a moment and shuddered. Then she told herself, *I have to.* She started forwards into the dark little space, coaxing Luna after her. "Come on, sweetheart," she murmured. "Come and sit in here. If there's beetles you can eat them up."

The little bear nosed in curiously, sniffing at the spongy wood and squeaking as dusty crumbs fell on her muzzle.

"I'll be back soon," Matthias said. "If I
can't find any tracks I'll come and shelter
with you and we'll wait till it's light. I'll
leave the pack here." He tucked it further
inside the hollow tree.

"Be careful," Hannah tried to call after
him but a huge yawn stole her voice away.

The hollow tree was fairly dry inside,
cushioned with powdery dead wood, and
wrapped in a snowdrift. It wasn't really

warm but it was so much cosier than being outside it felt blissful. Hannah curled up cross-legged, with most of Luna draped across her lap, her cold hands buried in her rough warm fur. She sighed and shuddered as some bits of dusty bark went tickling down the back of her neck. She was almost sure they weren't spiders…

"Matthias has gone to find you a new mum," she whispered to Luna, to distract herself from imagining little insecty feet. "I wonder how much you remember from before you were taken?"

Luna snuffled sleepily and Hannah rubbed her small round ears.

"She'll teach you everything, don't worry. You'll forget all about being shut up and the crowds and Benno. I promise." She yawned again. What time was it?

It felt as though they'd been walking for hours. It was the middle of the night, surely.

"Matthias will be back soon…" Hannah said wearily. "Any moment now…"

Then she was asleep.

※ ❄ ❊

She was woken by Luna, standing up on her lap and making a thin, worried growl.

"What is it?" Hannah asked thickly, trying to shake away her sleepiness. Where was Matthias? They must have slept a long time. She could see much more than she'd been able to when they'd first crept inside the hollow tree. It had to be morning already.

Outside she could hear a faint trampling sound, and then someone started to scrape and dig at the snow. Of course! He was back – that's what had woken the cub. Hannah wriggled up eagerly, patting Luna. "It's all right, shh, shh. It's only Matthias. Come back, Luna, don't be scared. I wonder if he's found the bear tracks. Hey, Matthias! Have you found her?"

There was no answer, only a strange, listening silence. Hannah blinked and yawned and tried to wake up faster. She felt dizzy and full of sleep. Why didn't Matthias answer her? Luna was still making worried little breathy growls and she was trying to back away further inside the fallen tree.

"Matthias?" Hannah had already begun to crawl forwards to look out of the opening they'd dug when she realized it might be someone else – a hunter, or someone out looking for firewood. Perhaps that was why Luna was worried, because it was a stranger.

Could the bear leaders have tracked us down after all? Hannah wondered, her stomach suddenly twisting with fear. For a moment she considered ducking back into the tree and then she remembered it was early morning. The gates of the city were probably still closed, with Jacob and Albert shut inside. How could it be them?

When she climbed out of the hollow tree, shaking herself and brushing away the snow, it wasn't the bear leaders staring back at her.

It was a bear.

Chapter
EIGHT

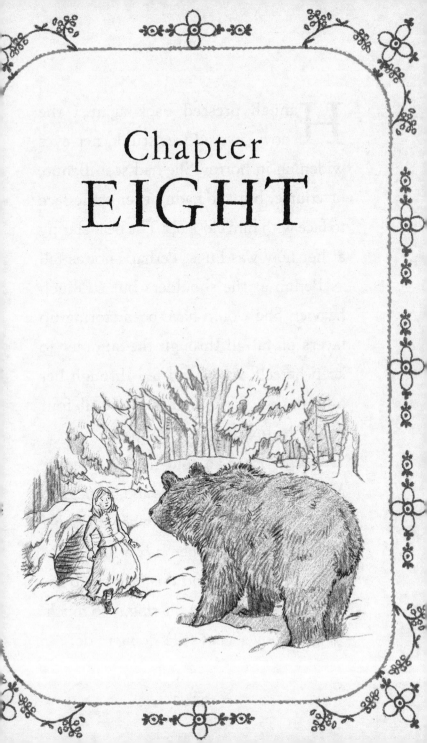

Hannah pressed back against the snow-covered tree trunk, her eyes widening in horror. She had seen Benno, of course, but she hadn't ever come face to face with him close up. The bear staring at her now was huge. Perhaps not as tall as Benno at the shoulders but so much heavier. She would have been storing up layers of fat all through the summer to keep herself warm and fed through her hibernation. Even standing on all four paws, she towered over Hannah.

Moths, Hannah told herself silently. *Matthias promised. Moths and beetles and mice. Not people. Except when a mother bear was defending her cub*, a little voice inside her added. *And this bear's cub has died and she must be missing it so much. So who knows what she's going to do?*

There was a tiny hiss from somewhere off to the side. "Hannah! Psst!"

Hannah rolled her eyes sideways to look at Matthias, standing against a tree trunk on the edge of the tiny clearing.

"Keep still!"

Hannah stayed fixed to the spot but she felt a little better, knowing Matthias was there. But what were they going to do? They had wanted to find the bear and now here she was. She certainly didn't look as if she was about to adopt an orphan cub, though. She was making strange huffing noises and smacking at the snowy ground with her paw. She seemed confused, maybe even frightened, but that didn't make Hannah feel any less scared herself. A frightened bear was a dangerous bear.

She looked sideways at Matthias again,

mouthing, *What do I do?* But he didn't seem to know. He stood by the tree, his fingers clenched into worried fists.

"Be ready to run," he whispered at last. "I'll see if I can distract her."

Hannah shook her head violently. She didn't want the bear to chase Matthias either! Then there was a scuffling noise and Luna scrambled out of the hollow tree, wearing a small mound of snow on her head, like a little hat. Hannah pressed her hand over her mouth to stop herself laughing. She looked so funny but there was a scared and angry bear glaring at both of them.

Luna stood staring at the mother bear for a moment and then she ducked her head, shaking off the little snow hat. The cub sat down on her haunches, looking away from the huge female, as if she was pretending the bear wasn't there. Hannah frowned. What on earth was the cub doing? It seemed so strange to ignore such a massive creature but it was working. The mother bear lumbered forwards, ignoring Hannah entirely, and bent her great head to sniff curiously at Luna.

Of course! Hannah realized. That's why she had come to the fallen tree – she must have been able to smell the cub. All that time Matthias had been looking for the bear, she had been looking for *them*.

Luna sat very still, letting the bear sniff her all over. Then she twitched in surprise as the mother bear began to lick her ears and muzzle, her long pink tongue sweeping over her fur. The bear was so absorbed that Hannah started to edge sideways towards Matthias.

The bear looked up sharply and Hannah froze. But she didn't seem to want to attack. She grunted and then swung round away from the tree. She set off across the clearing for a few paces and turned her head back to gaze at Luna. Then she grunted again, and made a noise that sounded to Hannah like her own mum clicking her tongue to get her to hurry up. *Come on then!* she was saying.

Luna stood up cautiously and followed the bear across the clearing. She did turn back for a moment to give Matthias and Hannah an uncertain sort of look. But then she bounded across the snow after the mother bear and pressed close in beside her as if that was where she'd always belonged. Hannah took half a step forwards, to follow them, then stopped. This was what they had wanted, after all.

She listened, straining her ears for their footsteps squeaking in the snow. The two bears disappeared among the trees and then there was silence. Just the faint whining of the wind.

Hannah stared after the bears, hardly able to believe they were gone. It had all happened so quickly. They'd spent ages worrying about how to rescue Luna and how to find her a new mother – and now it was done.

What does that mean for me? Hannah wondered wearily. *What happens to me now?*

"Are you all right?" Matthias demanded, running across the snow and grabbing her by the arms. "She didn't hurt you, did she? Hannah, talk to me!"

"I'm fine." Hannah tried to smile at him, even though she didn't feel like it. He looked so scared.

"I picked up her tracks by the river, where I'd seen her last, and I started following her. But it wasn't until she was almost at the clearing that I realized where she was going. I didn't know what to do!"

"You reckon she sniffed Luna out?" Hannah asked.

"She must have done." Matthias sighed.

"I suppose we should be happy. She's safe. She's got a mother again."

"I know, but…" Hannah's voice trailed off.

Matthias nodded. "I just can't believe she's gone." He crouched down and reached inside the fallen tree, hooking out his pack. Then he fished around inside and handed Hannah something wrapped in a piece of old, threadbare cloth. "Here. You'd better have this." He sniffed, his eyes glistening with tears.

Hannah opened out the faded cloth and saw that wrapped up inside was the wooden bear puppet. She stroked it with one finger. Every detail was perfect – the tubby little body, the spiky fur. "She looks happy," she whispered. "Happier than she did before, I'm sure of it."

Matthias looked down at the puppet.
"Maybe. When I first carved it, I was
remembering Luna scurrying up that tree
to get away from Albert and Jacob."

"And now we're thinking of her walking
off into the woods with her new mother."
Hannah wrapped the cloth back round
the puppet and tucked it inside her jacket.
"What do we do now?" she asked. She
didn't want to go – what if Luna came back?

But she knew the cub wouldn't.

"We found a new home for Luna," Matthias said slowly. "But what about you? We still don't know where you belong. Have you remembered anything?"

Hannah shook her head. Memories of her own time seemed almost like something out of a story. Luna and Benno and Matthias and the bear leaders seemed far more real than the hotel and the glittering lights of the Christmas market.

"Oh well…" Matthias shrugged the near-empty pack back on to his shoulders. "You'll just have to come back with me. My mother makes ointments and possets for everyone in our village. She'll know something to help recover scattered wits. Then when you remember, we can find your home." He glanced at her shyly.

"Or it wouldn't matter if you still don't remember. You could stay with us."

Hannah looked round at him in surprise and he gave a shrug. "I'd never have rescued Luna without you. We'll hopefully see her again in the springtime, you know. We'll be able to watch her grow up." Matthias smiled.

Hannah didn't know what to say. She loved the thought of being able to watch Luna – a wild bear roaming free in the forest. But she wanted to go home. She was tired and cold and her feet hurt, and she wanted Mum to cuddle her.

So she said nothing and followed Matthias through the trees, wondering what his mother would think when he brought home a stranger.

"Can you see the cottage?" Matthias

said, pointing. "There, through the trees."

Hannah couldn't see it when she first looked – the little house was half timbered, the walls painted white, with a framework of brown-black wooden beams. Surrounded by snow and dark tree branches, it seemed a part of the forest itself. Then she saw a faint thread of smoke idling up out of the chimney and sighed with delight. A fire! Warmth and hopefully a hot drink. She was still worried about walking into a strange house. But she could put up with anything if it meant she got to stand by a fire, and take off these soaking-wet shoes.

Matthias caught her hand and pulled her stumbling through the trees towards the cottage. He lifted the latch on the wooden door, and they tumbled inside a room that to Hannah's confused eyes seemed to be kitchen, bedroom and living room in one. There were children dashing about all over, at least two dogs and what looked like a chicken under the table.

A woman was sitting sewing by the fire, keeping an eye on a pot set in the embers. She sprang up as she saw them come in, dropping her sewing and running to hug Matthias. The children gathered to stare at them and the littlest clung to her mother's dress, sucking her fingers and peering up shyly at Hannah.

"You're back! Oh, we were so worried about you in that great snowfall yesterday. You should have stayed another night in the city." Matthias's mother held him at arms' length, looking him up and down, and then hugged him again.

"We found shelter when it started snowing hard," Matthias said, squeezing her tightly. "Mother, this is Hannah. I … I met her in the market. I brought her back here so you could help her. She doesn't know who she is."

Matthias's mother gave him a searching look, then beckoned Hannah towards her. "What do you mean, she doesn't know who she is?"

"Just that! She knows her name but that's all. She was begging and I got talking to her." He darted an apologetic sideways glance at Hannah but she didn't mind him twisting the truth a little. "I sold almost all the toys," he added, digging out a pouch of coins and pressing it into his mother's hand. "Here."

"Clever lad," his mother said, but she was still looking worriedly at Hannah. "Have you been ill, child? Have you had a fever? Or an injury? Did you hurt your head?"

"No…" Hannah whispered. "I don't think so." But the Christmas market and her parents and Olivia did feel like something she might have dreamed…

"Poor thing," Matthias's mother said, stroking her cheek. "But you're frozen!

169

You've been walking through the night, I suppose. Matthias, you shouldn't have made her do that. Here, sit down." She pushed Hannah gently on to the stool by the fire and poured water into a metal pot, hooking it over the flames.

"I'll make you a tisane," she said. "Warm your hands, girl. Take off that wet jacket, and those shoes. Look at the state of them! Matthias, fetch some blankets. Both of you had better get out of those clothes and sit by the fire."

Hannah leaned over, fumbling with the soaked straps that held her shoes on. Her fingers were so cold it took her ages to get the buckles undone. Then she stretched her feet towards the fire and watched her damp wool stockings begin to steam. She could hardly feel her toes but as the heat started to thaw them out they began to prickle and sting.

Flinching, she peeled off the rest of her wet things, hiding under the scratchy blanket as Matthias's little brothers and sisters giggled and whispered to each other. It sounded like they were daring each other to talk to her. Matthias's mother handed Hannah what looked like a shirt with a drawstring neck to wear and she wrapped herself tightly in the blanket.

"Poor frozen child," Matthias's mother murmured. "What were your people thinking? Surely someone must be out looking for you… Here, drink this." She pressed an earthenware cup into Hannah's hands, wafting steam and a sharp scent of herbs. "Whatever shall we do with you?" she asked, gazing at Hannah and shaking her head. "Finish up that drink – you look half asleep." She nodded towards the bed built into the far side of the room, with a curtain hanging across it. "Get some rest, go on."

Hannah nodded and smiled exhaustedly, scurrying across the stone floor. She was glad to dive behind the curtain, away from the staring children. Perhaps they could tell she didn't belong? She curled up tightly, huddling the blanket round her shoulders, and stared at the threads woven into the curtain. She could hear Matthias's mother questioning him quietly about where he'd found her and who she might belong to.

"She'll remember where she came from," she heard Matthias say. "I know she will. Or if she doesn't, couldn't she stay here with us?"

I can't stay here... Hannah thought sleepily. *They're kind and I'd love to see Luna again in the spring with Matthias but I want to go home to my own family...*

"Hannah, are you still cross with me?"

Hannah yawned. Had she been cross? She didn't remember. She peered up at her little sister, who was sitting on the end of her bed, gazing at her anxiously.

"I know it was my fault your bear got broken. I'm really sorry. You can have some of my holiday money if you like. Or you can have some of my lolly."

Bears… Hannah blinked and then sat up, looking round the hotel room in confusion. She had her snowflake pyjamas on again. The bed was soft, with a cosy duvet on top, not scratchy blankets.

"It's OK," she murmured. "I'm not cross. I had such a strange dream."

Olivia hugged her. "Can I get in with you? It's too early to get up and my feet are cold." She scooted under the duvet and leaned her head on Hannah's shoulder. She was almost as wriggly and warm as Luna, Hannah thought, half lost in her dream.

"Oh! You mended him. How did you do that?"

Hannah saw that Olivia was looking at the bear puppet, which was sitting on the table, propped up against the lamp.

Did I buy it from the old man at the Christmas market? Or did Matthias carve it and give it to me? Or maybe … both? The bear's front paw was stuck back together again. There wasn't even a splinter where it had been broken at the arm joint.

"Magic..." Hannah said, smiling to herself, and Olivia rolled her eyes.

"I'm glad it's mended, anyway. Did you take the collar off?"

Hannah swallowed hard. She stroked the back of the bear's neck, feeling fur under her fingers again. There was a faint paler ring on the paint, where the red clown ruff had been.

"Yes. The bear didn't like it," she muttered. "So Matthias took it off."

Olivia peered round at her. "Who? You're still half asleep!"

Hannah nodded. "Probably..."

"It's a very beautiful bear," Olivia said, yawning.

"Yes, she is. A beautiful, funny, wild bear..." Hannah whispered back, hugging her little sister tight.

Turn the page for an extract from

STAR

by HOLLY WEBB

"Do you really think it will snow?" Anna whispered as soon as Mr Ford's back was turned. They were supposed to be reading, but most of the class had at least one eye on the window and the patch of yellowish-grey sky they could see over the wall of the playground.

"Definitely," Ruby hissed back. "It's so cold. And it just looks like snow, doesn't it?"

Anna nodded. There was something about that scrap of sky. It looked heavy, as if the clouds were filled with snow. Just in time for the end of term tomorrow. It would be perfect. She peered over her page at the clock – surely it was home time by now? Usually she loved ending the day with reading, but the thought of snow made it too hard to concentrate.

When the bell rang at last, there was a second of complete silence and then everyone leaped up, cramming books and pencil cases into their trays and racing for the cloakroom.

"If it snows like it's supposed to, maybe we won't even have to come to school tomorrow," Ruby said hopefully.

"The last day's always fun, though!" Anna said, wrapping a scarf round her neck. "Mr Ford said we can watch a DVD after lunch. But that's not as much fun as playing in the snow," she admitted.

"Exactly! Come on, let's go and see if it's started yet!"

Anna and Ruby hurried out into the playground to look at the sky. It was a dark, dark grey now, but there were still no snowflakes.

"Do you think the forecast has got it wrong?" Ruby said, peering at the clouds.

Anna sighed. "I hope not."

"It will snow, *zvezda moya*, don't worry."

"Baba!" Anna turned to hug her grandma. "I forgot you were picking me up today. Mum's going to her office Christmas party and Dad's working," she explained to Ruby. "I'm staying over at Baba's house tonight."

Ruby nodded. "What does *zvez* – whatever your baba said mean?" she whispered.

"It's Russian for 'my star'," Anna explained. "It's just a nice thing to call somebody. Baba, do you really think it's going to snow?"

"Definitely. Those are snow clouds.

If it doesn't start before you go to bed tonight, you will wake up to a white world tomorrow, I'm certain. Now –" she looked thoughtfully at Anna's bag – "do you have everything? Your mama dropped a bag off with me this morning, but she said to make sure you had brought everything home. Homework? PE kit?"

"No homework and I've got my PE kit." Anna waved it in front of her.

"See you tomorrow, Anna! My mum's calling me." Ruby dashed away and Anna slipped her hand into Baba's.

"Can we watch a film together tonight?"

"Mmm, I should think so. You can find me a nice Christmas film. I made those honey cookies you like. We can have some when we get home."

They walked back to Baba's house,

admiring all the Christmas lights and
decorations on the way. Anna liked
the sparkling reindeer standing on her
neighbour's lawn.

"We're going to put up our tree this weekend. Have you got a tree yet, Baba?"

"My little tinsel tree is in the loft, but I haven't got it down yet. Perhaps you can help me put it up later. But it feels early to me, to be putting up a tree. Christmas is weeks away," Baba grumbled, and Anna laughed.

The church in Russia worked on a different calendar, so Christmas Day wasn't until January 7th. There would be all the New Year celebrations first. Anna loved the party that Baba always had for all her Russian friends on New Year's Eve.

"You could always have Christmas twice!" Anna suggested.

"Two Christmases! Certainly not." Baba shook her head, pretending to be cross. "What an idea. You know, your cousins in Russia won't be on their school holiday until the day before New Year's Eve."

Anna sighed. "I bet Tatiana and Peter and Annushka have got masses of snow."

"Oh yes." Baba smiled. "But nothing like a year or so ago, when they had that huge snowfall. Do you remember? Two months' worth of snow fell in one night and Uncle Michael had to dig out their front door."

"I wish we could go and visit them again," Anna said enviously. "But in the winter, this time. We could go to Russia for New Year! I'd love to see really deep snow. Here it's just cold." She shivered. It was definitely a lot colder than it had been the day before.

They hurried into Baba's little flat, and

Baba made a cup of tea for herself and hot chocolate for Anna. Dipping the spiced honey cookies into the hot chocolate, Anna started to feel her frozen toes again. "This is nice, Baba," she murmured. But she couldn't resist looking round to check out of the window for snow.

"It will come, Anna! I promise. Let's go and watch our film, hey?"

It was lovely, snuggled up on the sofa. Anna almost forgot about the snow. She was starting to feel really Christmassy now.

What should she get Baba for Christmas, she wondered as the film ended and Baba went into the kitchen to heat up the soup she'd made for dinner. Baba loved little ornaments. She had lots of them on the shelves in her living room

– animals and dancing girls and baskets of flowers. Perhaps she could buy her grandma a special new one?

"Anna, switch it over to the news, please," Baba called from the kitchen. "I like to know what's going on. I can hear it from here."

Anna changed channels and went on looking at Baba's ornaments, wondering whether she had enough pocket money to buy something really nice. Then something the newsreader said caught her attention, and she yelped with excitement.

"What is it?" Baba asked, popping her head round the door.

"Look! It's Vladivostok! That's near where Tatiana and Peter and Annushka live, isn't it? It's on the news!"

"I'll turn the soup down." Baba hurried

back into the kitchen and then came to sit with Anna. "What's happening? Is it the snow again?"

"No! They're saying there's a tiger in the city!"

"Oh my… I don't believe it." Baba peered at the screen, gasping at the blurry footage of a tiger – a real tiger! – racing across a busy road.

One special bond. One incredible adventure.

STAR

From best-selling author
HOLLY WEBB

THE
SNOW
BEAR

FROM BEST-SELLING AUTHOR
HOLLY WEBB

The
Reindeer
Girl

FROM BEST-SELLING AUTHOR
HOLLY WEBB

THE
WINTER
WOLF

FROM BEST-SELLING AUTHOR
HOLLY WEBB

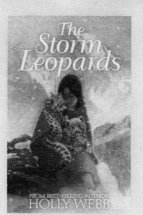

The
Storm
Leopards

FROM BEST-SELLING AUTHOR
HOLLY WEBB

The
SNOW
Cat

FROM BEST-SELLING AUTHOR
HOLLY WEBB

THE
STORM
DOG

FROM BEST-SELLING AUTHOR
HOLLY WEBB

One special fox. One amazing journey.

FROST

From best-selling author
HOLLY WEBB

HOLLY WEBB

Holly Webb started out as a children's book editor and wrote her first series for the publisher she worked for. She has been writing ever since, with over one hundred books to her name. Holly lives in Berkshire, with her husband and three children. Holly's pet cats are always nosying around when she is trying to type on her laptop.

For more information
about Holly Webb visit:

www.holly-webb.com